Nursery & Playtime Rhymes

Wendy Straw's

From Hey Diddle, Diddle (page 24)

Wendy Straw's
Nursery & Playtime Rhymes

Illustrated by Wendy Straw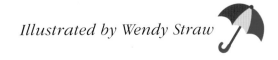

BROLLY BOOKS

Brolly Books

an imprint of Borghesi & Adam Publishers Pty. Ltd.

Suite 330, 45 Glenferrie Road

Malvern Vic 3144 Australia

Tel +61 3 9533 8863 Fax +61 3 9533 8843

Email emma@brollybooks.com

www.brollybooks.com

First published as a series of 5 individual books titled

The Wheels on the Bus (2000), Five Little Ducks (2001), Old MacDonald had a Farm (2002), Humpty Dumpty and
Friends (2003), and Incy Wincy Spider and Friends (2004)
by Borghesi & Adam Publishers Pty. Ltd.

This cased edition first published 2005.

Illustrations by Wendy Straw

Copyright illustrations ©Wendy Straw, 2005

Copyright this compilation ©Borghesi & Adam publishers, 2005

Original text for The Owl and the Pussycat by Edward Lear. The text as it appears in this edition is an abridged version.

Printed in China

Cataloguing-in-publication data is available through the
National Library of Australia

ISBN 1 877035 64 5

CONTENTS

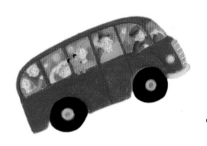

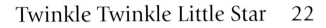

The Wheels on the Bus

The wheels on the bus
go round and round,
round and round,
round and round,

The wheels on the bus
go round and round...

All day long...

The driver on the bus
goes beep beep beep,
beep beep beep,
beep beep beep,

The driver on the bus
goes beep beep beep...

All day long...

9

The people on the bus
go up and down,
up and down,
up and down,

The people on the bus
go up and down...

All day long...

The wipers on the bus
go swish, swish, swish,
swish, swish, swish,
swish, swish, swish,

The wipers on the bus
go swish, swish, swish...

All day long...

13

The wheels on the bus
go round and round,
round and round,
round and round,

14

The wheels on the bus
go round and round...

Bus Depot

Until the day is gone.

Humpty Dumpty

Humpty Dumpty sat on the wall.
Humpty Dumpty had
a great fall.

16

All the king's horses and all the king's men
Couldn't put **Humpty** together again!

The Owl and the Pussycat

(from Edward Lear)

The Owl and the **Pussycat** went to sea
In a beautiful pea-green boat,
They took some honey, and plenty of money,
Wrapped up in a five-pound note.

The **Owl** looked up to the stars above,
And sang on a small guitar,
'O lovely Pussycat! O Pussycat, my love,
What a beautiful Pussycat you are.

Baa Baa Black Sheep

Baa, baa, black sheep, Have you any wool?
Yes, sir, yes, sir, **Three** bags full.

One for my master,
One for my dame,
And one for the **little** boy
Who lives in the lane.

Twinkle Twinkle Little Star

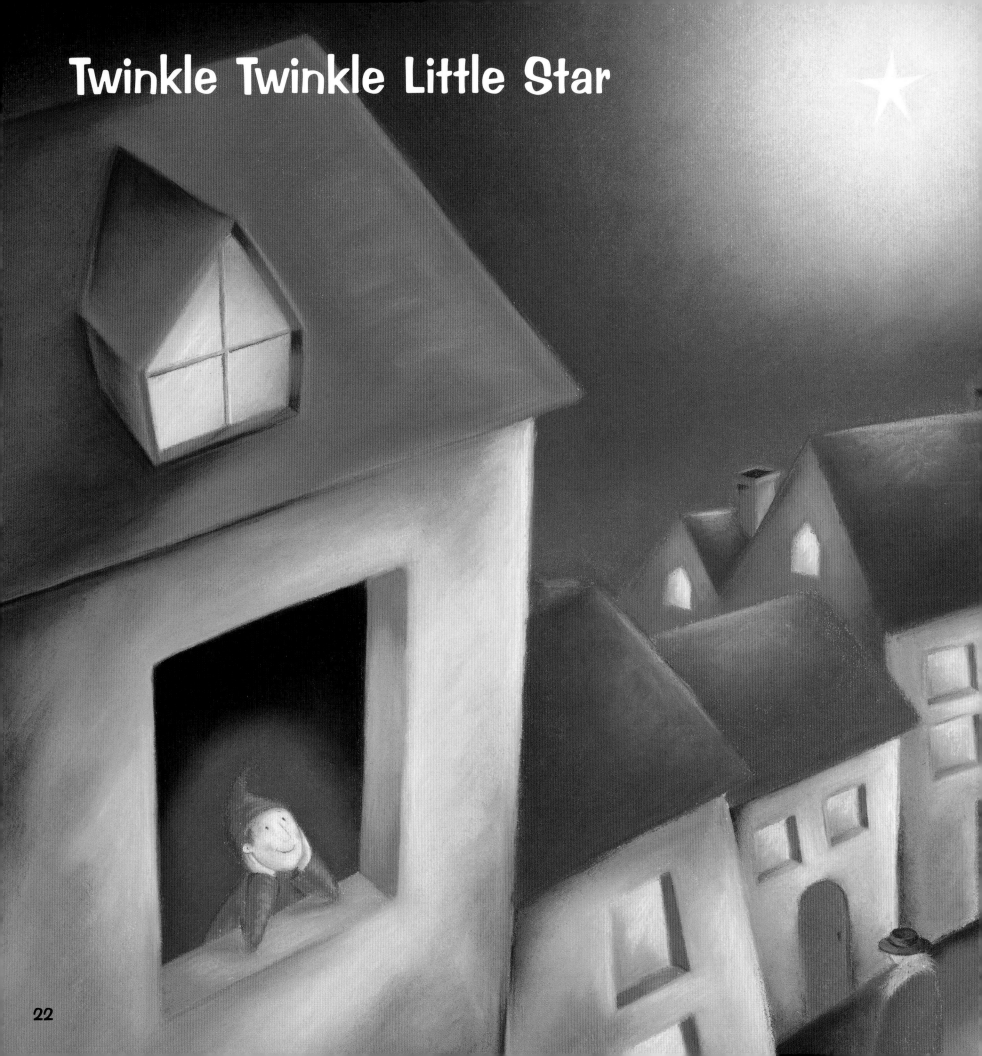

Twinkle, **twinkle**, little star, How I wonder what you are.

Up above the world so high, Like a diamond in the sky.

Twinkle, twinkle little star, How I **wonder** what you are.

Hey Diddle Diddle

Hey diddle diddle,

The cat and the **fiddle**,

The cow jumped over the moon.

The little dog laughed,
To see such fun,
And the **dish** ran away with the spoon.

25

Old MacDonald had a Farm

Old MacDonald had a farm,

EE-I EE-I O

and on that farm he had some ducks,

EE-I EE-I O

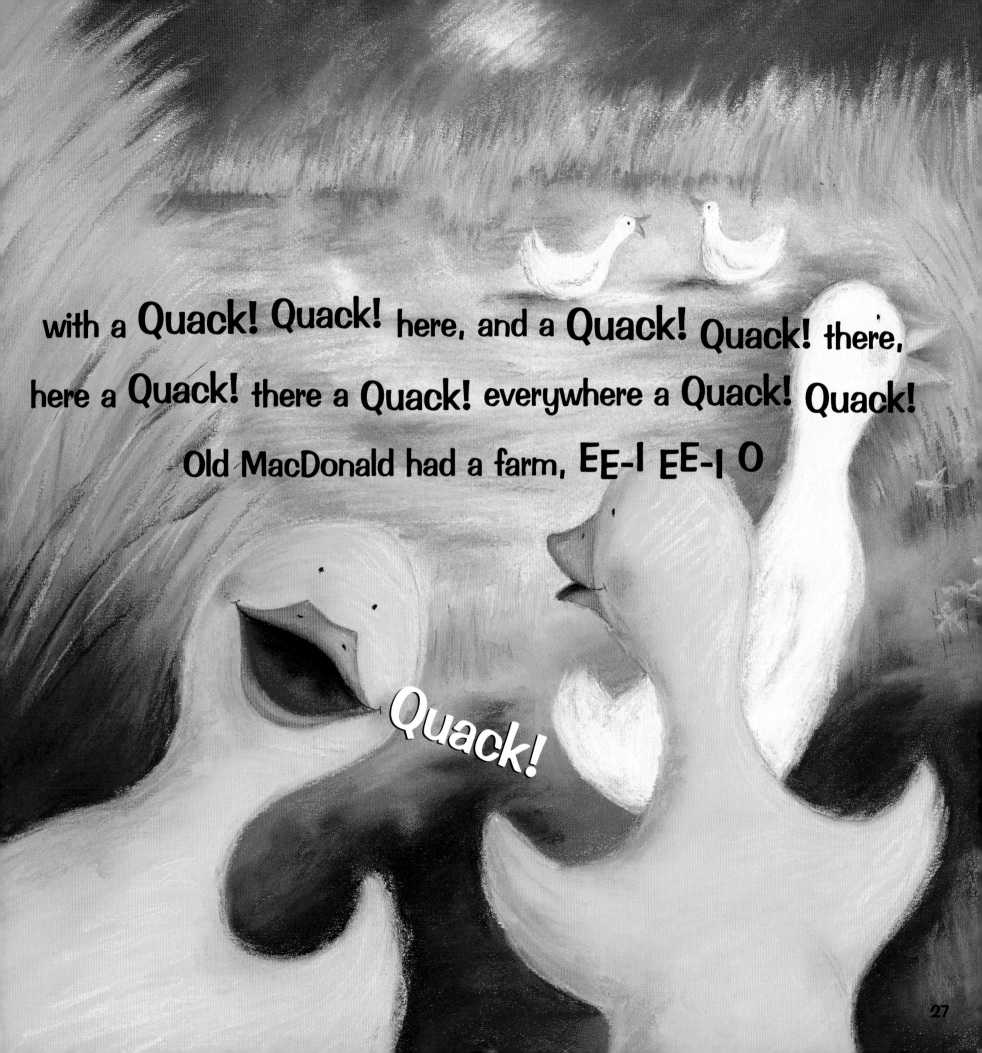

with a Quack! Quack! here, and a Quack! Quack! there,
here a Quack! there a Quack! everywhere a Quack! Quack!
Old MacDonald had a farm, EE-I EE-I O

Quack!

...and on that farm he had some cows,

EE-I EE-I O

with a Moo! Moo! here, and a Moo! Moo! there,
here a Moo! there a Moo! everywhere a Moo! Moo!
Old MacDonald had a farm, EE-I EE-I O

...and on that farm he had some pigs,

EE-I EE-I O

with an **Oink! Oink!** here, and an **Oink! Oink!** there,
here an **Oink!** there an **Oink!** everywhere an **Oink! Oink!**
Old MacDonald had a farm, EE-I EE-I O

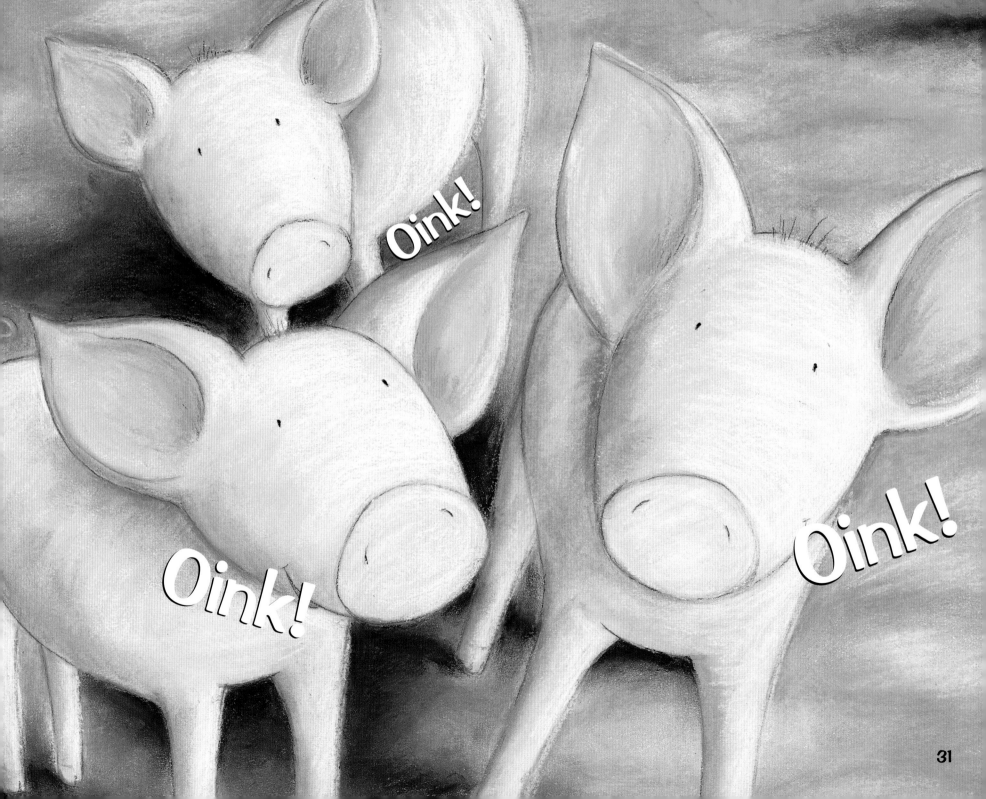

Oink!

Oink!

Oink!

...and on that farm he had some sheep,

EE-I EE-I O

with a Quack! Quack! here, and a Moo! Moo! there,

Moo!

Moo!

Oink!

Quack!

Baa!

Baa!

here an Oink! there an Oink! everywhere a Baa! Baa!

Old MacDonald had a farm, EE-I EE-I O

Incy Wincy Spider

Incy **wincy** spider climbed the water spout,
Down came the rain and washed poor **incy** out.

Out came the **sunshine** and dried up all the rain,
So incy wincy spider climbed the **spout** again.

Five Little Speckled Frogs

Five little **speckled** frogs sat on a hollow log
eating some most delicious bugs... **yum yum**

One **jumped**
into the pool
where it was
nice and cool.
Then there were four
green speckled frogs
... **glub glub.**

continue counting backwards as follows

Four little speckled frogs ...

Three little speckled frogs ...

Two little speckled frogs ...

One little speckled frog ...

and now there are no green speckled frogs... glub glub.

Once I Caught a Fish Alive

One... **two**... three, four, five,
Once I caught a fish alive.
Six... seven... eight, **nine**, ten,
Then I let him go again.

Why did you let him go?
Because he bit my **finger** so.
Which finger did he bite?
This **little** finger on my right.

41

Noah's Ark

The **animals** went in two by two,

Hurrah! Hurrah!

The animals went in two by two,

Hurrah! Hurrah!

The animals went in two by two,
Tigers, lions and zebras, too,
And they all went in
For to get out of the rain.

43

Row, Row, Row your Boat

Row, **row**, row your boat,

Gently down the stream.

Merrily, merrily, **merrily**, merrily,

Life is but a dream.

Aaaaahhh...

Row, row, row your boat,
Gently down the stream.
If you see a **crocodile**,
Don't forget to scream.

45

Five Little Ducks

5 little ducks went out one day
over the hills and far away.

Mother duck called
Quack! **Quack!**
Quack! Quack!

but only four little ducks came back.

4 little ducks went out one day
over the hills and far away.

Mother duck called
Quack! **Quack!**
Quack! Quack!

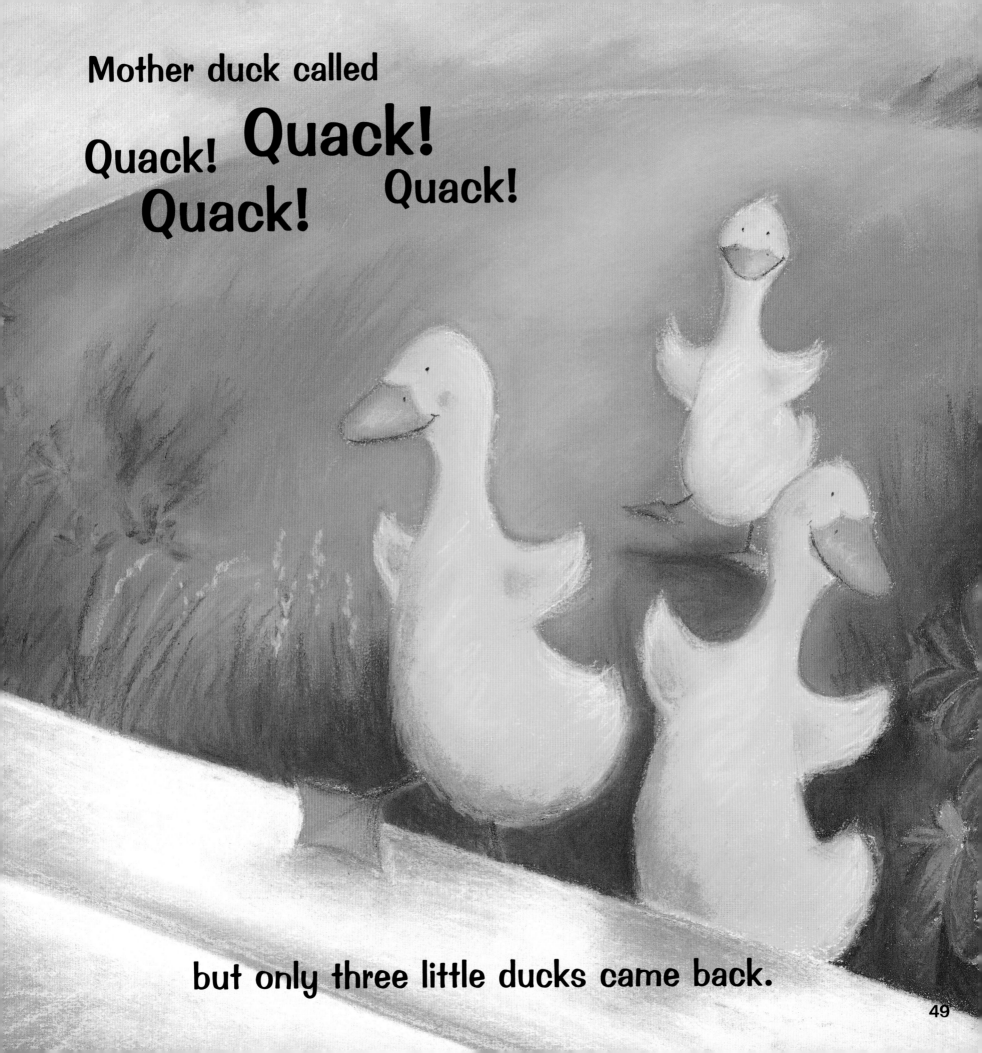

but only three little ducks came back.

3 little ducks went out one day over the hills and far away.

Mother duck called

Quack! **Quack!**
Quack! Quack!

but only two little ducks came back.

2 little ducks went out one day
over the hills and far away.

Mother duck called

Quack! **Quack!**
Quack! Quack!

but only one little duck came back.

1 little duck went out one day over the hills and far away.

Mother duck called

Quack! **Quack!**
Quack! Quack!

and all her five little ducks came back.

Hickory Dickory Dock

Hickory Dickory Dock,

The mouse ran up the clock,

The clock struck one,

The mouse ran down,

Hickory Dickory Dock.